CHAPTER ONE

Lewis sat at the bar of the empty pub, a shot of Bell's whisky in front of him and a bulging rucksack at his feet. A cigarette burned in an ashtray, he stared at it for some time, at the fiery red tip and the blue smoke rising towards the ceiling, before taking a last drag on it, mashing it out in the ashtray and gulping the raw whisky which burned his throat. He coughed and looked around him, at the empty pub where he'd worked for nearly three years. At the beer-pumps he'd pulled, at the optics he'd emptied and replaced a thousand times. At the cigarette machine, the fourth since he'd started working there – the first three having been damaged beyond repair by kicks or crowbars worked up inside them to get at their contents. At the sticky carpets and yellowed walls bearing pictures of the Queen.

Time to say goodbye to it all. Time to let it go.

He got off the stool, leaned down and hoisted the rucksack onto his back, grunting at its weight. Who'd've thought that money could be so heavy? It's just paper. As he turned to go he saw the pub door reflected in the mirror behind the bar swing inwards and a stocky baseball-capped figure come in.

'Closed,' Lewis said. 'Sorry. Don't open till eleven.'

'Oh what a shame,' said the figure and Lewis, with a heavy heart, recognized the voice. 'A man can't even get a drink in his own fucking pub. Terrible state of affairs, that. Something should be done.'

'Cakes,' Lewis said with surprise. 'Today's only Tuesday. Wasn't expecting you til tomorrow.'

'Need some money, don't I? Got a bit of business needs sorting out. The none-of-*your* kind of business, before you ask. What's in the rucksack?'

Jonathan 'Cakes' Cunningham; so called because, as well as the Queen's Head pub they were standing in, he owned a bakery and that's how he moved his drugs around London, hidden in confectionery. Couriers would drive cream sponges across the city, hollowed out inside and filled with powder. Or boxes of éclairs concealing clingfilm-wrapped bundles of pills. Shaking, skinny, spotty people would come into the bakery and purchase doughnuts

BRING IT BACK HOME

NIALL GRIFFITHS

ACCENT PRESS LTD

Published by Accent Press Ltd – 2007
ISBN 1905170912/9781905170913
Copyright © Niall Griffiths 2007

The Quick Reads project in Wales is a joint venture between the Basic
Skills Agency and the Welsh Books Council. Titles are funded through
the Basic Skills Agency as part of the National Basic Skills Strategy for
Wales on behalf of the Welsh Assembly Government.

Printed and bound in the UK

Cover Design by Emma Barnes

at ten or twenty pounds each, a small envelope hidden where the jam should be. And as well as the bakery and the pub and the drug dealership, Cakes also owned a group of men loyal to him and the wages he paid them. All of them would happily use knives, even guns, on anyone Cakes told them to. And as well as the bakery and the pub and the gang of vicious men, Cakes also owned a terrible temper, a black rage that made him famous around King's Cross. People would whisper that he knew where bodies were buried. That he'd put them there. There was a rumour that Cakes once used his bakery's mincing machine to dispose of a victim, and the sausage rolls and pasties from there tasted very strange for a month or so. An old granny, enjoying her meat-and-potato pie lunch, had chipped her tooth on a wedding ring. Such were the stories that were attached to Jonathan 'Cakes' Cunningham.

'I said, what's in the rucksack?'

Lewis's mouth had dried up. His hands were shaking slightly.

'Just some washing,' he said. 'Machine's on the blink. Need to go to the laundrette.'

Cakes ducked under the bar flap and disappeared. Lewis knew what he was doing; he was opening the safe which was set in the floor behind the bar. Except he wouldn't, at the moment, need the combination.

'Ah well,' Cakes's voice came up from behind the bar. 'Make sure you're back for opening time. On the fucking dot. I heard that you were late opening yesterday and – '

There was a half-empty bottle of Bells on the bar. Lewis reached for it and held it by the neck like a weapon.

'– and that means I lost money. And if there's one thing I hate it's losing money. It'll come out of your wages. I...Why's this safe open? Where's the fucking money gone?'

Cakes rose up from behind the bar and as soon as Lewis saw his baseball cap he brought the bottle down onto it, as hard as he could. It didn't break but there was a terrible THUNK noise. Lewis felt the impact in his shoulder and Cakes went back down behind the bar as if shot. Lewis raised the bottle again and waited for Cakes to re-appear and when he didn't he leaned over the bar to look. Saw Cakes, on his back, his eyes rolled to show the whites. For a horrible moment Lewis thought he might be dead, but then he saw Cakes's chest rising and falling so he dropped the bottle and hoisted the heavy rucksack back onto his shoulders and ran.

He made for the nearest tube station but suddenly it seemed very far away so he hailed a taxi instead. He could afford the fare, now, and could even afford to leave a tip for the driver at Paddington station where he bought a ticket, one-way, for the next Swansea train. It wasn't leaving for an hour, so he went into the station bar and bought a pint of lager and a whisky nip and sat in the corner facing the door so he could see who came in. His hands shook as he raised the drinks to his lips and they only stopped shaking after four drinks: two pints and two whiskies. The rucksack he held on his knee, protecting it with an arm as he might protect a child. His knees twitched. He chainsmoked cigarettes and drummed on the tabletop with his fingertips and his nerves screamed. He thought of sausage rolls that dripped blood. He thought about cutting into a pie and finding his own eyes staring out at him. He thought of Cakes, big man Cakes, and his fury when he regained consciousness, and when the Swansea train was announced over the tannoy Lewis ran onto it and found a seat. Only when it began moving was he able to relax again. As he moved out of London he felt himself calming down. Felt his heartbeat returning to normal.

NIALL GRIFFITHS

He took out his mobile phone and tapped a number into it. The Old Man answered.

'Hello?'

'It's Lewis. I'm on the train and I'm coming home. I'll be there in a few hours.'

'You okay, son? You sound upset.'

'I'm okay.'

'You sure? You don't *sound* okay. What's wrong, boy?'

'Nothing, nothing. I'm fine. I've just...'

'Just what?'

'Nothing. I'll tell you when I get there. In a few hours.'

'Okay, son. Bring yourself back home. It's been too long.'

'I've just...'

'It's okay, Lewis. Whatever it is, bring it back home and we'll sort it out.'

Lewis hung up and sat back to stare out of the window. The Old Man's voice echoed in his head, which was spinning due to the booze. He thought of green hills and small white houses. He thought of his mother's gravestone in the churchyard on the hill that overlooked the village – he thought of his brothers and he thought of Manon. More than anything he thought of Manon, her skin and her smile and her eyes. He thought of Cakes and the Queen's

6

Head pub and London and how happy he was to be going away from all of that. He'd never go back there again.

Tiredness came on him. His eyes started to close. He put the rucksack on his knee and wrapped one of its straps tightly around his wrist. He leaned his head against the window and closed his eyes. By the time the train reached Reading he was fast asleep, dreaming of the place he was aiming for, the place he still called home.

CHAPTER TWO

'Can you believe it? He hits me – *me* – over the head with a fucking bottle. He's taken every last penny from the safe and fucked off and I know where he's gone – back to bleedin' Wales. Taffland. Mark my words. Can't believe the fucking cheek of him. Thinks he can get away with this, does he? With *this*?'

Cakes removed his baseball hat and leaned to show the raised lump on his shaven skull. The size of a plum beneath the skin. Same colour as a plum, too. The three men around him looked and tutted. One of them, the one the others called Daft Larry, touched it gently; Cakes yelled and leapt back.

'Fuck's sakes, Larry! I didn't say to *touch* the fucking thing, did I? How fucking stupid *are* you? See how you like it, eh?'

Cakes grabbed Larry in a headlock, picked up a rolling pin from the counter-top and thwacked it hard four times on Larry's skull. Larry screamed loudly. Cakes let him go and he scurried into the corner by the bread-slicing machine. He crouched down behind it, holding his head in his hands, and whimpered.

Cakes regarded him with disgust and shook his head and then looked up at the other two men, Scottish Jim and an older man called Smith. Smith was carefully inserting small bundles of plastic-wrapped pills into hollowed-out scones.

'I'm sorry for what happened and the boy needs to be taught a lesson right enough,' Scottish Jim said, 'but what do you want us to do about it?'

'Do? It's not what I *want* you to do but what you're *going* to do. Both of you.'

'And that is?'

Cakes leaned back against the fridge and picked up a Bakewell tart. He bit into it and pulled a face. He spat half-chewed pastry out onto the floor and then threw the rest of the tart at Daft Larry who howled again and shrunk further into the corner.

'Tastes like shit. No sugar in it. Who made that? That brain dead dickhead over there?'

Smith shook his head. 'No. I did. You never said anything about making the cakes *taste* good, boss. I mean, nobody's going to *eat* them, are they? Not *this* batch, anyway. And sugar costs money. That's what you said.'

Cakes stared at Smith until Smith looked away and then he said:

'Right. This is what's going to happen. I'm going to Wales to find that thieving bastard Lewis. It'll take me –'

'How will you do that, boss?'

'What?'

'How will you find him? I mean, how'd you know where he lives?'

'Oh, I'll find him, don't you worry about that. I'll find the fucker. Follow him to the fucking moon if I have to. But it's going to take me a couple of days, and in the meantime here's what you're going to do.'

He reached into his pocket and pulled out a piece of paper.

'You're going to bake me a wedding cake. Big one, three tiers, loads of icing. Little bride and groom on the top of it. Here's a list of the ingredients. Special ingredients.'

He gave the list to Jim and both he and Smith read it together. Smith gave a low whistle and Jim raised his eyebrows.

'You sure about this?'

'Never been surer.'

'I mean, this is a lot.'

'I know that. Got to make it worthwhile, tho', Jim, haven't I? Got to cause a *lot* of trouble. Not going all the way to Wales to just mess about, know what I mean?'

'Okay. You're the boss.'

'And don't you *ever* fucking forget it.'

Cakes pointed at the piece of paper in Jim's hand.

'At the bottom of that list is an address. I want the cake delivered to that address at three in the afternoon on the day after tomorrow. Understand?'

'How can we do that?' said Smith. 'Post Office can't guarantee time of delivery, can they?'

'Then use Parcelforce or something, shit-for-brains. Jesus, pay a fucking cabbie to take it if you have to. I don't care as long as *that* cake gets to *that* address at *that* time on *that* day. Three o'clock, day after tomorrow. Understand me? Do what I pay you to do.'

Both men nodded. Cakes went on:

'Don't fuck up. 'Cos if you do I'll come back and I won't be carrying a bag of flour. '

He picked a bag of self-raising from the counter-top and held it up in his hand to show the two men, then he threw it, with force, at Daft Larry. It struck the bread-slicing machine and burst and Larry howled again as the white powder covered him and turned him into a cringing ghost. Cakes again shook his head in disgust and left the bakery. He got into his van, started it up and headed westwards out of London.

CHAPTER THREE

Lewis got off the train at Swansea, stood on the platform and stretched and yawned. People scurried past him and the accents they spoke in were pleasing to his ear; such a relief to hear them after the years of hard Cockney in King's Cross, or the hundred languages that weren't variants of English spoken there. He had a cup of tea and a KitKat in the station cafe as he waited for the Carmarthen train. When he was on that train he gazed out the window at the passing scenery and the expression on his face was a contented one. He got off at Ferryside and then caught a bus that took him up into the hills. He got off in a small village by a garage, streams of sparks lighting up the dark workshop. He took his rucksack into that dark workshop and a man in greasy blue overalls stepped out of the shadows beneath a car up on jacks. His teeth looked very white in his oil-streaked face as he smiled. Lewis and this man leapt at each other and hugged and Lewis yelled:

'Robat! Brother!'

'Aw Christ, Lewis. The Old Man said you were coming. Great to see you. Is everything okay? What brings you back?'

'I'll tell you later. Where is he?'

'Who?'

'The Old Man.'

'He said to call him when you got here. You give him a ring and I'll go and get us all a bit of dinner.'

Robat left the garage and Lewis called the Old Man. When Robat returned with bags of food from the chipshop, they set up a lunch table in the garage office – a pot of tea and a plate of white sliced bread, salt and vinegar and ketchup and four packets of fish and chips. The third brother, Marc, soon appeared and greeted Lewis with a hug and a slap on the back and as they sat down to eat the Old Man appeared too. He stood at the end of the table with his big beard and halo of thin hair shining whitely in the gloom. He and Lewis did not hug, they merely exchanged nods.

'Hello, son. Journey okay?'

'Yes.'

'That's good, then.'

They sat and unwrapped their food parcels and steam rose in a vinegary whiff. Lewis poured four mugs of tea and passed them around. Hands reached out and took slices of bread and folded them around chips. The ketchup bottle was passed around and squeezed and dispensed sauce four times with four farty noises. The men ate in silence. Only their slurps of tea and wet chewing sounds hung in the oily air. And the slight cracking noises as they broke crisp batter on fish with the edges of forks.

After ten minutes or so the Old Man crumpled his empty wrapper into a ball, burped and sat back in his chair. He linked his hands across his bowling-ball of a belly that pushed out at his faded checked shirt. He worked a piece of food out from between his front teeth with his tongue and chewed it and swallowed it. He stared at Lewis. Lewis stared back and then looked away. A shred of golden batter was caught in the Old Man's beard like a fly in a web. He said:

'Lewis. Here he is back from London with his tail between his legs, no warning, no explanation. Tell me now, boy – should I be worried, or what?'

Robat and Marc stared at Lewis. They both took packets of tobacco out of their breast pockets and rolled cigarettes, even though the

Old Man tutted in disapproval at their doing so. Lewis shook his head.

'I don't think so, no. They're never going to find me here, are they? All they know is that I'm from Wales. They haven't got a clue where I live.'

'"They"? And tell me, who are "they"?'

'Well, Cakes Cunningham and his boys. Y'know Cakes? Remember me telling you about Cakes back when I first started working for him?'

The Old Man nodded. 'The feller with the bakery and the pub?'

'That's him. It's not *just* a bakery, tho'...'

And Lewis told his family about Cakes's illegal operations, about the drug-running, and about the violence that he was willing to use on those who threatened his business. About Scottish Jim and old Smithy and Daft Larry, a mentally-retarded young man whom Cakes treated as a kind of clown or dog to taunt and kick when he was frustrated. And he told them about stealing Cakes's money and what he was intending to use it for – but he didn't tell them about needing to whack Cakes over the head with a whisky bottle. That seemed to be a detail that his family didn't need to know about.

They listened to Lewis's tale in silence and

expressed no surprise, which surprised Lewis, in turn. Then the Old Man sighed and rubbed his hand across his face.

'I knew no good would come of it,' he said. 'Didn't I, boys? Didn't I say no good would come of it all?'

He looked at Marc and Robat who murmured and nodded in agreement but did not look at Lewis. Like twins they studied the ends of their cigarettes and Lewis reached for his tobacco on the table and rolled one too. The Old Man tutted again.

'But, listen,' Lewis said. 'It was you who told me to go to London in the first place. After that stuff with Manon, remember? You told me to get out of the village. Go and disappear in the city. That's what you said.'

'Yes, and why? Because Manon's dad was on the bloody warpath. He was going to tear you limb from limb and feed you to his pigs. It was for your own protection. Getting a sixteen-year-old girl pregnant, what were you thinking of?'

'Aye, well, it's not like I did it deliberately. And anyway I wasn't much older than that meself, was I?'

'That's beside the point, son. Whether it was an accident or not, that's neither here nor there. How *old* you were is irrelevant as well.

17

Fact is, you had to leave the village. And then when Manon miscarried…Christ, her father was looking for you with a shotgun. A bloody shotgun, boy. Told him you'd run away I did, that none of us had the first clue where you'd gone. Didn't we, boys?'

Nods and murmurs again.

'He would've shot you. He would've killed you. You had to go.'

'Wasn't me he ended up shooting, tho', was it?' Lewis said.

Three heads were shook. Lewis asked: 'They had the autopsy yet?'

'Accidental death,' Robat said. 'Seems like he was cleaning his gun or something and forgot it was loaded and…'

'Bang,' Marc said. 'Blew his own brains all over the barn. Lucky Manon never found him. That would've killed her.'

'Could've been suicide of course,' Robat said. 'No-one really knows. He never left a note, tho'.'

'Who was it found him?' Lewis asked. 'You never told me in any of your texts. Just said he was gone, like.'

'One of his farmhands,' Marc said. 'What a thing to find, eh? First thing of a morning as well. Jesus.'

Marc shook his head sadly at the thought of it all. All four men sat there thinking in silence for a couple of minutes and then the Old Man said:

'So that makes Manon an orphan. Which you three will be as well if this old feller doesn't get a few whiskies inside him in the next half hour or so. Pub's just opened. Welcome home, Lewis son.'

Lewis put his rucksack in the locker and they all went over the road to the Miner's Arms which was already busy. Lewis was warmly greeted and bought several drinks; it seemed to him that the unpleasantness with Manon had been forgotten. The people were prepared to forgive around here, he thought, and he very quickly began to feel as if he'd never left. He and his family sat at a table by the window out of which he could see right across the valley with the thick mist rising from the trees on the far side. He could see the quartz in the rock on the hilltop catch the fading sunlight. A sense of being at home, of being safe, came into him. He was with his brothers and his father and his old friends in the place he still called home, and everything was going to be okay.

They drank. They started to laugh. The sky grew dark outside and stars began to shine. The barman drew the curtains and shut the outside world from view. Round about the sixth pint the Old Man's mobile phone rang; he looked at his screen and pressed 'answer'.

'I've got to take this, boys. Could be important...' he slurred and went outside, the phone to one ear and a finger in the other.

Robat fetched more drinks from the bar. When he returned he told Lewis that he'd just received a text from Manon and showed him the screen:

> Tell lewis meet 2moro noon
> at cemetry. Manon xxx

Lewis nodded and Robat pressed 'delete'. Lewis picked up his fresh pint and drank half of it in one gulp. He was happy. He was home.

CHAPTER FOUR

Cakes got hungry in the early afternoon just outside Swindon, so he left the motorway and pulled into the car park of some ugly brick bunker of a pub called the Traveller's Rest or something like that. A big, brown building with a small playground – seesaw, swing and slide – now empty and drizzled on. An annexe called the Wacky Warehouse, obviously closed now, pool tables and fruit machines dead and unlit inside. 'Two for a fiver' meal offers hung above the door of the pub itself which seemed overlit and garish and loud. And above it all roared the traffic on the motorway, exhaust fumes drifting down from above in a thin rain of grey soot.

An uninviting place, but Cakes was hungry. Wanted something hot. He parked and went into the pub and approached the bar. The spotty lad behind it made a movement as if he was doffing an invisible hat.

'What?'

'Take your cap off please, sir.'

'What?'

'Can you take your cap off, please.'

'Why?'

'Company policy. No hats allowed.'

'Why not?'

The lad shrugged. 'Don't know. It's just company policy.'

Cakes sighed and removed his cap and rubbed his palm across the stubble on his skull. It made a rasping noise.

'Satisfied?'

Another shrug. 'I don't make the rules, sir. It's company –'

'Policy, yeah, I know. You've already said. I need to order some food.'

'Menus are on the table, sir. Order at the bar with your table number.'

'And I need a pint of lager.'

The barman poured a pint of Foster's. Cakes took it over to a window seat and sipped at it. Warm and flat. Soapy, almost. Like run-off from a washing machine. He studied the menu, a pointless exercise really because cheeseburger and chips was the only thing he fancied. He gave his order at the bar and paid, then returned to his seat. He sipped again at the lager. Warmer. Flatter. Soapier. Fruit machines whooped and bleeped and coughed out coins, and several TV screens set high up on the walls showed some middle-aged and be-suited men in a studio talking, probably about sport of some kind. Several tables in the pub were occupied by families or couples, but there was very little conversation; the people seemed happy to simply sit in their seats and eat their food and drink their drinks and stare into space or up at the TV screens or at the walls – anywhere but at the person sitting next to them. Signs around the pub exhorted people to have fun. One sign advertised the 'FREAKY FRIDAY!' approaching, when bottles of Breezer would be two-for-one and house vodka fifty pence a shot.

Cakes scanned the faces in the pub, searching for a pretty one, or one with an unusual scar or birthmark – anything interesting or distracting. There were none – all were bland and expressionless. One blonde woman was mildly diverting until she happened to smile at her overweight child and Cakes saw her teeth, broken and brown and rotten. Not even the TVs offered entertainment since the volume on them all was turned right down – and what pleasure or point is there in watching a few blokes in suits having a bit of a natter? Can't even hear what they're saying, so there's nothing to disagree with. So what's the point in having the television on at all? The soundtrack was the noise of the fruit machines, whoopwhoop and bleepbleep and kachunkakachunka. Cakes couldn't stand it. He'd leave as soon as possible, after he'd eaten his food and drunk his pissy pint.

The food came. A handful of white chips and a burger in a bun that would be gone in two bites. A limp shred of lettuce and a slice of wrinkled tomato. Cakes looked around for cutlery and condiments and saw none, so he went back up to the bar.

'Knife and fork? Salt and vinegar?'

The spotty lad wordlessly pointed at an array of cutlery and sachets of sauces. Cakes took a knife and a fork and some packets of salt and pepper and vinegar and one of red sauce too. He squeezed them over his food back at the table and began to eat.

The chips were pale and uncooked. Tasteless. Frozen to begin with and still cold in their centres. They left a film of slime on the inside of his mouth after he swallowed them. He bit into the burger. Also cold, also slimy. The processed cheese slice was unmelted, so uncooked was the meat, and when Cakes sniffed at the burger he thought he caught a whiff of something stale, sweetly rancid. He took the plate up to the bar and showed it to the barman.

'A problem, sir?'

'I can't eat this. It's cold. And horrible.'

'I'll have a word with the chef, sir.'

'I'm not gonna eat raw burger and chips.'

'I said I'll speak to the chef, sir.'

The barman took the plate into the kitchen and came back out.

'Chef will heat it up for you, sir.'

Cakes went back to his table. Some minutes later the food came back. It was steaming hot but drooping and soggy; evidently it had simply been put into the microwave for a couple of minutes. The red sauce Cakes had squirted on the chips was bubbling hot, and when he tried to spear a chip it slid off his fork and broke apart on the plate. When he bit into the burger, heated grease spurted out onto his hands. The pathetic slice of tomato scorched his tongue and he spat it out. What was on his plate he wouldn't feed to a dog. In fact, even a starving dog would turn its nose up at it. And seven quid! For *this* shit! Disgraceful. Absolutely disgraceful.

He wiped his hands on a napkin and bundled it up. He dumped it on the sweaty mound of chips and left the pub. Outside, he scanned the lamp-posts and walls for surveillance cameras and saw none, so he went over to the knee-high wall that bordered the car-park and studied it for loose bricks. He couldn't see any so he repeatedly kicked the top layer with the sole of his shoe until one brick came loose and then he worked it back and forth with his hands until it broke free. He lifted it in his right hand then walked back over the car-park and threw the brick through one of the pub windows, hurling it overarm, with force. An alarm immediately screeched and people screamed and scattered and Cakes calmly climbed back into his van and reversed out of his parking space. The spotty barman and a fat chef wearing a white apron and checked trousers came out of the pub, the chef carrying a large knife. As Cakes sped past them he gave them the finger and laughed at their stupidly gawping faces. Too stupid even to check out his number plate. Faces with the simple, empty features a child might draw on a balloon.

Cakes re-joined the motorway, and some miles down it he pulled into a service station where he topped up his tank and bought a ham salad roll, a bag of crisps and a can of lemonade. He ate in his van and flicked through an old copy of the *Daily Mirror* that he found on his dashboard. Kylie Minogue diagnosed with breast cancer. Something about the Beckhams snapped shopping in Tokyo or somewhere.

He took out his mobile and tapped in a number.

'Hello?'

'It's me, Cakes.'

He heard pub sounds on the other end of the phone; voices and laughter. He heard an old man's voice say something about having to take the call because it could be important and then he had a conversation with that old man, evidently outside the pub because the voices in the background had ceased talking and the old man could talk quietly. Then Cakes put his phone away and re-joined the motorway again, heading west.

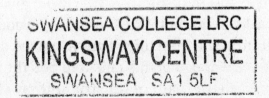

CHAPTER FIVE

Up in the cemetery that overlooked the village the wind blew hard and cold, whistling and whining around the gravestones and the church tower, and through the trees and long grass. Lewis turned his face into it and hoped that it would blast the hangover out of his head. Which, to an extent, it did. When his eyes were watering uncontrollably and his face felt as if it had been slapped twenty times or so, he turned his back on the wind and sought shelter in the church doorway. He sat on the stone bench there, icy cold on his arse, and looked out.

The entire village could be seen from the churchyard. Lewis could trace the route of his growing up: the cottage hospital where he was born, the school he attended, the Old Man's garage, the pub, the bus stop from where he caught the bus out of the village – he could see it all from the cemetery, high up on the hill. He could see the big old oak tree on the green opposite the pub with the mossy bench underneath it where he first kissed Manon, and he remembered, now, that first kiss; how his heart thumped, how his pulse raced. The way her lips and breath tasted of cider and cheese and onion crisps, and how happy he felt and grateful to her for wanting to be kissed by him. He remembered the way she arched her head back to meet his lips with hers. How that movement exposed her throat, the creamy white skin and the sharp, small bulge of her Adam's Apple. That's when he'd fallen in love with her, he thought, at that precise moment, when she offered him her throat. He fell head over heels in love with her then. And, really, he'd loved her ever since.

He checked his watch: 11:53. She'd be here soon. Always punctual, Manon. If she said she'd be somewhere at midday she'd be there at midday, not 11:59, not 12:01. You could set your clock by her.

And the field behind the oak tree where they'd had sex, not ten minutes after that first kiss. The field where he'd gotten her pregnant. It had been summer then; they'd both been very young, and the field behind the oak tree had been full of golden corn. Lewis had used his shirt for a sheet among the corn and he and Manon had made a kind of nest in the tall yellow stalks. Neither of them could control themselves. It had been the first time for both of them but it came naturally; they knew what to do as if they'd been doing it for years. Their excitement overrode any concerns about contraception, and anyway where were they going to get condoms from? The chemist was closed and he was too young for the pub. He'd thought about sneaking in the back door and using the machine in the toilets, but someone was bound to see him and then the next day the Old Man would've wanted to know why he'd needed contraceptives. By the time this scenario had played itself out in his head Lewis had ejaculated and gone limp inside Manon and had rolled off her. Both of them were panting on their backs in the corn, staring up at the night sky, at all the summer stars. It had almost been magical. Lewis had heard many people say that their first time was a big disappointment but his wasn't, oh no.

Then Manon's period was late. In fact, it never came. And the curse of living in a small village became apparent; Mrs Price the chemist noticed that Manon hadn't been in to buy any tampons or sanitary towels and, having a mouth on her the size of the disused mine up the valley, began the rumour of Manon's pregnancy. A rumour which was true. So

Manon hid herself away, barely leaving the house, wearing baggy fleeces – even though it was summer – to hide her growing tummy-bump. Her father demanded to know what was wrong with her and she told him she felt ill so he called out Dr Watkins who, of course, could find nothing wrong with her. She and Lewis made plans to run away. To Cardiff. To London. To New York even, the cities getting bigger and further away, big and far enough to swallow them so that they'd never be found and they could build a life together, just the two of them and the baby when it came. But then the blood came instead, one night when they were sitting on the swings in the playground and planning their escape; Manon stood up off the swing and noticed that she'd left a little pool of blood there. She quickly became hysterical and Lewis called the Old Man who came and took them both to hospital in his car. Manon was whisked away very quickly and Lewis and the Old Man were left alone to wait, so the questions began: 'What's going on, son? What's happening to that poor girl? What have you done to her? You stupid little bastard! What's her father going to say?'

A white-faced doctor came to see them and used the words 'miscarriage' and 'internal bleeding'. He knew Manon's father and telephoned him, so the Old Man took Lewis back home. Then he went back to the hospital and while he was there Lewis fled. First he called a friend in London, asked him if he could stay with him. Then he packed some clothes. Then he gathered up all the money he could find in the house, every last penny, and he caught the bus to Carmarthen. Then he caught the train to Swansea and then another one to London. He stayed with his friend and found a job in a pub owned by a dodgy character called Jonathan Cunningham, also called Cakes. That job paid the rent on a bedsit Lewis found. He worked there for some years until one day he got a text from his brother telling him that Manon's dad had died, so a plan grew in Lewis's head. He stole a lot of money from one seriously dangerous individual who he whacked unconscious with a whisky bottle and fled again, this time towards his home. Now he sat on a cold stone bench and waited for Manon to appear in a windswept churchyard overlooking the village.

And there she was. Just standing in front of him and smiling as if that was where she belonged.

'Hiya, Lewis.'

He stood up to greet her. Felt his face split in a smile. She was wearing a black woollen overcoat and black mittens and her face was flushed pink, both from the wind and the exertion of the walk up the hill. Her hair was as black as a crow's breast and her eyes as brown and shiny as horse chestnuts fresh from the shell. She looked exactly as Lewis remembered her – utterly beautiful.

He didn't know whether he could hug her or not, and his arms felt useless at his sides. She stood on tiptoe to kiss his cheek and then they both went back into the shelter of the church doorway. He felt warmth coming off her. Smelled the soap in her skin and the shampoo in her hair. He took out his tobacco and offered it to her. She shook her head. He put the tobacco back in his pocket. Asked Manon how she was.

'Well. Not too bad, considering.'

'Yes. I'm really, really sorry about your dad, Manon. Dead, dead sorry. It must've been awful.'

She gave him a small, sad smile and shrugged. 'It was. Still is. What made it worse was that I hadn't seen him in ages. We kind of drifted apart just after...you know, that thing...'

She looked at Lewis and he nodded. The nod told her that he understood and that she should continue to speak. She took a crumpled tissue out of her overcoat sleeve and wiped the end of her nose with it.

'And of course the village was too small to avoid him, so I moved to Swansea for a bit. Stayed with friends from school.'

'Why'd he do it?'

'Who?'

'Your dad. Why'd he, like, shoot himself? I mean if it wasn't an accident, like. It wasn't because of me and you and what happened, was it?'

Manon shook her head. This movement dislodged a lock of her hair which fell down over one eye and she delicately brushed it back with her long fingers. It was a gesture that made Lewis start to fall in love with her all over again.

'He'd been depressed for quite some time. All his life, really, he'd struggled with depression, off-and-on, like. And then he found out that he had liver cancer and he didn't have long to live. And his only daughter was away in London...'

She looked at Lewis out of the corner of her eye. It was a look that suggested something like guilt.

'London? You said Swansea.'

'Yes, Swansea most of the time but I've got friends in London as well, so I spent a lot of time there. Holborn, that area.'

'Holborn? Aw Christ, I was dead close, in King's Cross. Why didn't you tell me? We could've met up.'

'We'd split up, Lewis. You ran away and left me in the hospital. The point was *not* to meet up with you, don't you think? The point was to *avoid* you.'

'Suppose. Surprising we didn't bump into each other, tho'.'

'Is it? In London? A city with three times the population of the whole of Wales? It's not surprising at all we missed each other.'

Lewis kept quiet. He could sense that Manon was getting annoyed. He didn't know why, but knew that he didn't want to irritate her further so he said nothing and just let her talk.

'I met some interesting people in London, had some good times,' she said. 'I was going to stay there but I had to come back here for the reading of Dad's will, so...'

'D'you think you'll go back?'

'To London?'

'Yes.'

'Maybe. Dunno. Dad left me everything – the house, his car, his savings, the lot. If I stay here, I'm quite rich. If I sell it all off and go and live in London I'll be just a little bit well off. Have to live miles out, in Mill Hill or somewhere. Don't think I'd like that. But then there's nothing for me here so I don't know what to do, really.'

Lewis looked back out over the village. Manon's words boiled in him; what had she been doing in Swansea and London? Who had she stayed with? Who had she met? Who had she slept with? He hated to think of her having a life that didn't include him. The urge to hold her and kiss her was almost irresistible. She was sitting so close to him; he could smell her and feel the heat from her skin yet she seemed so very distant, with her stories of a life in two cities that he'd never been a part of. For the first time Lewis regretted leaving Manon in the hospital with an intensity very like pain; it was like a stab in his chest. He'd been terrified, both of Manon's father and, to a lesser extent, of the Old Man – but he should've acted like a man and stayed by her side. He should've been brave. Should've toughed it out. Shouldn't've run away to bloody London and left her there in hospital having lost a baby and her bloody father in a rage at the end of her bloody bed.

Well, never again. Lewis would make amends. It's never too late to change things around, he thought to himself.

'Manon,' he said.

'What?'

'Come with me. I want to show you something.'

'What is it?'

'You'll have to come with me.'

'Where to?'

'Just over there. Come on.'

He stood and automatically held out his hand for Manon to take. When she didn't, he put it back in his pocket, somewhat embarrassed. Manon followed him across the graveyard, around the huge yew tree to the Garden of Rest and the big marble headstone there.

'It's your mother's grave,' Manon said. 'I've been here before.'

'I know that, yes. But look.'

Lewis reached behind the gravestone and pulled out his rucksack from where he'd hidden it earlier. It was under a fallen yew branch and, he believed, protected by the spirit of his mother. He held it in his arms and unzipped it, tipping it forwards slightly so that

Manon could see inside. She looked. Her eyes went wide and her mouth fell open.

'Thousands of pounds, Manon,' Lewis said. 'Thousands. With this and what you'll get from selling off your dad's stuff, we can go anywhere. Remember what we spoke about when we found out that you were gonna have a baby? About running away? Cardiff and London and New York? Well, fuck it, let's go to New York. Let's get married and buy an apartment in New York somewhere. Just me and you, eh? And this time we'll *really* have a baby. Start a family. What d'you reckon? Say yes. Please say yes. Marry me, Manon. Please.'

She looked away from the money and Lewis's face. He reclosed the sack and slung it over his back.

'Jesus, Lewis. This is too quick. I don't know what to do. Or say.'

'Say yes.'

She looked back at him, into his eyes. Her eyes were dark, with sparks flashing in their depths. Lewis realized that he was, at the moment, asking too much.

'Okay. I'm being unfair, expecting an answer right away. But tell me you'll think about it, yes? Overnight. You'll think about it overnight, will you do that?'

She thought for a moment as if she was making some calculation in her head. She nodded. 'Okay. And we'll meet in the back room of the pub tomorrow. In the afternoon.'

'What time?'

'About half past two.'

'Alright.'

'But I can't guarantee *anything*, Lewis. Can't guarantee I'll say yes. I'll have to think about it and talk to certain people and loads of things. I need time on my own. This is all too...'

She waved her hands in the air in a gesture that indicated confusion and chaos. Lewis understood and backed away from her.

'I need time,' she said. 'Don't call me or anything tonight, okay? I'll see you tomorrow afternoon.'

Lewis nodded and stepped aside, watching her walk away. He watched her leave the cemetery. Heard her mobile phone ring and saw her take it out of her pocket and speak into it:

'Hello? Oh, it's you. Where *are* you?'

She left the graveyard still speaking into the phone, heading down into the village. Lewis watched her until she'd turned the corner out of sight and wondered who'd been calling her. Wondered who'd been on the other end of the phone.

She hadn't asked him where he'd gotten so much money from, which was strange. Maybe his proposal had startled her so much that she'd forgotten to ask. Or maybe she thought he'd saved it. Did it matter? Lewis crouched down at the side of his mother's grave and asked her if it mattered. Asked her also if he'd done the right thing, if asking Manon to marry him had been sensible, and honourable. He asked his dead mother lots of questions and if she answered, if he heard her voice in the earth, then it was heard by no-one but him.

CHAPTER SIX

In the early afternoon Cakes entered the outskirts of Bristol. He pulled off the motorway onto a large estate, parked by a row of shops and then called a number on his mobile phone. He had a quick conversation with the person on the other end who asked him where he was and then gave him some sketchy directions which Cakes scribbled down on the back of a crumpled envelope. Then he bought fish and chips and ate them in his van, then he bought a *Daily Sport* at the newsagent's and got back in his van and drove back onto the motorway. He followed the signs for the nearest Travelodge and found it just as the streetlights were flickering on, dusk arriving early there. A few minutes later and he was sitting on the bed in a hired room, sipping tea, telly on. He turned to the back pages of the *Sport* and scanned the list of 'Escorts' there. One caught his eye: BUSTY BRISTOL AREA H/H VISITS, and a phone number which he called on his mobile. A female voice answered, husky with cigarettes:

'Hello?'

'I'd like to see you tonight,' Cakes said. 'In about an hour. Can you do that?'

'Where are you, lover?'

Cakes told her. Then asked: 'How much do you charge?'

'Depends on what you want, doesn't it? But we can talk about that when I get there. In about an hour.'

'Okay.'

'I need your room number, darlin'.'

Cakes told her. 'There's a side entrance,' he said. 'So you don't have to go through reception.'

'I know the place. See you in about an hour.'

'Great.'

He snapped his telephone shut and finished his tea. He then took a shower, scrubbing himself from head to toe, brushing his teeth, shaving his face and shampooing the stubble on his head, hissing with pain as he rubbed the blue lump on his skull. He cursed Lewis, and then cursed himself for not packing a smart set of clothes as he put back on the outfit he'd set off in that morning: t-shirt, denim jacket, sweatpants, baseball cap, all of which smelled slightly sweaty, so he gave them, as well as his armpits, a blast of Lynx. Then he went downstairs to the bar where he sat and drank a few pints of lager on his own, watching the people come and go, come and go. He wondered what they were doing there, in that Travelodge on the outskirts of Bristol. Were they on a mission like him? Were they just visiting the city, to shop or sight-see? Or were they due to catch flights from the nearby airport? They were all a mystery to him.

On the way back to his room Cakes saw a sign saying 'CRECHE', with an arrow pointing down a corridor. He followed that arrow and found himself in a small room containing a silent riot of beanbags and spongeballs, soft sticklebricks and other children-entertaining things, but no children. He noticed a stack of board games in one corner and went and shuffled through them, choosing the Connect 4. Back in his room he set the game up on the floor, between the bed and the window. He made another pot of tea. Turned the telly on and sat down to wait.

Three soft knocks on the door. Cakes opened it with what he hoped was a welcoming smile. The ad hadn't lied; 'busty' was an accurate description. She was big all over.

'This is the right room, lover, yes? You called me earlier?'

'Oh yes,' Cakes said. 'That I did. Come in. Want some tea?'

He stepped aside and she tottered in on extremely high heels. Put her handbag on the bed, took her scarf off and put that next to the handbag. Cakes could feel the night air coming off her, see the goosebumps raised on the bare skin of her arms and legs, uncovered as they were by the tiny denim skirt she hardly wore.

They looked at each other. She was a large woman with a heavily made-up face. Lots of black hair – probably extensions, thought Cakes – piled up on the top of her head. Lots of jewellery. Big dark eyes in circles of vivid green eye shadow, and pink lipstick applied seemingly an inch thick. Cakes wanted to ask her to remove some of the make-up but he would've felt rude doing so, so he just asked her again if she wanted some tea.

'It's already made,' he said. 'It's in the pot.'

'Okay then.'

He poured two cups and she sat on the bed and removed her shoes, sighing with relief. She massaged her toes and her soles, the dinges in her skin where the shoe-straps had cut in. She noticed the Connect 4 screen on the floor.

'What's this?'

'What?'

'This, here.'

She pointed to the game with a bare big toe, the nail painted crimson. Cakes handed her the tea.

'Well, I thought we could have a game or two,' he said. 'Just pass the time, y'know?'

'Ah, I see.' She blew on and sipped her tea. 'You're, erm, lonely, right? Travelling or something and you just want some company, is that it?'

'That's about it, yes.' He sat down crosslegged on the floor facing her, the Connect 4 between them. 'Is that okay? D'you mind?'

She slid off the bed so that she too was sitting on the floor, facing Cakes. 'Not at all, lover. It's your money. And this is one of my favourite games.'

'Good.'

And so they played. She won the first game, and the second, which were played in silent concentration. As Cakes was re-setting the board for a third game she asked him where he was going, what he was doing in Bristol.

Cakes shrugged. 'I'm on my way to Wales.'

'Holiday, is it?'

'No. I'm looking for someone.'

'Oh. I won't ask what for, then.'

'Best not.'

'Will he, erm, be happy to see you, this person?'

'You're asking a lot of questions.'

'I'm sorry. Just curious.'

Cakes smiled. 'Well, it's a good question – which I won't answer. But I bet he'll be *surprised* to see me. I don't doubt he'll be surprised. He thinks I don't know where he is. But, y'see, I *do*.'

Cakes laughed then, a small, soft chuckle to himself, almost under his breath. 'Oh yes. I *know*.'

The woman looked at him. She listened to him chuckling to himself and watched him set the game up, watched his fingers, the vigour of his movements. She was looking for aggression. Was he a danger to her, this odd man who only wanted to play Connect 4 and drink tea? Was she in a bad situation, here, with him? No, she didn't think she was. She'd been in this business for several years and she'd learnt how to tell within two minutes of meeting someone whether they were a threat to her or not. It could be seen in their eyes, in their movements, in their laughter – too quick to laugh or too slow to laugh, both were danger signs. But this man, here...he seemed okay. She felt safe. Her prostitute's sixth sense was telling her so. There was a certain hardness in him, she didn't doubt that, and she pitied whoever it was he was hunting, but she could sense no menace towards herself in this man. He just wanted to play Connect 4. And drink tea.

So they played on, game after game. She was very good at it and whenever she won, as Cakes's counters would clatter to the floor, she'd clap the soles of her feet together in an innocent, girlish way. Cakes liked her doing that so he started losing on purpose. She was good company and he didn't want her to go.

Round about midnight he got tired. It had been a long day, and driving long distances always exhausted him. The adrenalin rush of putting the brick through the pub window had long since left him drained and weary. He told the woman he wanted to go to bed and asked her how much he owed her. She closed her eyes and moved her lips as she made a calculation in her head and then she gave Cakes a figure.

'Okay,' he said. 'Just let me get my wallet.'

He stood. She remained seated, on the floor. He stood still for a moment, thinking.

'What's up, my lover?' she said, looking up at him.

He looked down at her. 'How much for a blowjob?'

She gave him a price. Cakes unbuttoned his fly. She laughed to herself and thought: *Too good to be true. It always is.*

CHAPTER SEVEN

When Lewis was a little boy, about ten years old, the Old Man – who wasn't so old then, of course – taught him a hard lesson. He stood Lewis upright in the centre of the garage office; he stood behind him and told the boy to fall backwards. *Just relax and let yourself go*, he said. *Just let yourself fall backwards. I'll catch you. Trust me, boy.*

And so little Lewis did exactly that; he imagined he was a tree in the forest and toppled backwards, knowing that the Old Man would catch him and lower him gently to the floor or softly steer him back upright with his strong and reliable hands.

Except the Old Man didn't catch him. He just stood aside and watched as Lewis thumped against the floor, the air being jolted out of his chest with a yelp. And as little-boy-Lewis lay there sobbing, winded and shocked, trying to get his breath back with whooping gulps of air, the Old Man leaned over him with his eyes hard and his mouth un-smiling in the beard which was then just beginning to grow white and wild and he said:

'That's your lesson, son. Never trust anybody. Remember this day for the rest of your life. Trust no-one.'

It had been a cruel lesson, and Lewis remembered it clearly as he walked down into the village from the churchyard on the hill. He remembered the shock, the humiliation, and the huge disappointment. Had it been an important lesson? Had it been valuable for life? Lewis wasn't sure. All he knew was that, sometimes, he *hadn't* been betrayed by those he loved most – his brothers, say, or Manon – but that *he* had betrayed *them*. Or he'd betrayed Manon, anyway. Betrayed her terribly. So, really, Lewis reflected as he went into the garage and stowed the rucksack safely in the locker again, the lesson should've been: never trust yourself. If an opportunity arises for you to act like a coward and betray your own heart, you'll take it. Never trust yourself.

Cakes – he'd also betrayed Cakes. Not the same as betraying Manon of course but, well...Cakes had trusted him. How foolish of the man.

Lewis's expression was sad as he left the garage and went over the road to the Miner's

Arms. It was half-full of people having an after-work drink or two and Robat and Marc, still in their oil-stained blue overalls, were at the fruit machine. Lewis bought them a pint each and then took his own drink into the corner, where the Old Man was sitting over a large Scotch and reading the local paper.

'Ah, Lewis. Sit down, son.'

Lewis sat. The Old Man neatly folded the paper and placed it on the seat beside him.

'You look unsettled, Lewis. What's wrong?'

Lewis told him about his meeting with Manon, about making a kind of peace with her, about his proposal of marriage, but he left out the detail of possibly fleeing to New York with her. The Old Man listened intently to Lewis's words, sipping at his whisky, shaking his head in disapproval when Lewis rolled a cigarette. When Lewis had finished speaking the Old Man drank the last of his Scotch and put his elbows on the table. He leaned over it towards Lewis and said:

'So this bothers you, does it? What you asked Manon to do, you're having second thoughts about it now, are you?'

Lewis shook his head. 'Not at all. What's bothering me is that she'll say no.'

'When're you next meeting her?'

51

'Tomorrow. Back room, here, half past two.'

The Old Man stared at Lewis. He dug his fingers into his candy-floss beard and scratched at the chin that was hidden somewhere in there. Then he said:

'The barman here, you know him?'

Lewis nodded. 'Course I do, yes. He's worked here for ages.'

'And d'you see the young man at the pool table over there? With the white shirt on?'

Lewis turned to look and nodded again.

'Well, he's the barman's son. Only neither of them know that. The barman met a woman twenty years ago, bang, she gets pregnant, buggers off without telling him. Has the baby, a boy, puts it up for adoption. The foster family live in this village, so the baby comes back to where he was conceived. The woman – the mother, like – knows this, but thinks it best to say nothing about it. So there they are, father and son, except neither knows the other. They speak to each other every night, aye, but it's only to ask for another drink or a bag of bloody peanuts. What d'you make of that?'

Lewis shook his head. The Old Man went on:

'And d'you see the fat feller at the end of the bar, with the bag of pork scratchings? Well, he doesn't know it, but he's got a half-sister in

Bristol. Nothing unusual there, no, except she's on the game like and every month or so that man goes to Bristol to see her. To have sex with her. He's been doing it for years – paying his own half-sister to have sex with him.'

'Jesus Christ.' Lewis shook his head. 'How d'you know all this?'

'I know the mother. The man's father was a docker in Cardiff, the daughter's dad is a welder from Merthyr. But they share the same mother. Who I know. She'll never tell them that they're related 'cos it would destroy them. Imagine that: you find out that you've been paying to have sex with your half-sister. For years. That news would just about kill you, wouldn't it?'

Lewis nodded. 'Why tell me all this, tho'? What's the point?'

'What, these stories? No point really, except to show you that everything's connected. In ways you'd never dream of. There are enough secrets in this village alone to make a library full of books, boy. We're all mysteries to each other but we're all linked to each other, too. Everything's connected. D'you know what I mean?'

Lewis gave no answer. Just sipped his lager.

'Ah, you'll find out for yourself, soon enough,' the Old Man said. 'But everything's connected. Remember that, son. In ways you'd never dream of. The links are everywhere. You've just got to learn to look for them.'

The Old Man's words were coming out a little slurred and Lewis realized that he was a bit drunk. Probably been in the pub all afternoon, drinking whisky, that's why he was talking gibberish. Just rambling, that's all the Old Man was doing. Not making much sense. Interesting stories, but did they mean anything to Lewis? Was there a point in telling them? Christ, the whole world was a soap opera.

Robat and Marc came over with a tray of drinks and soon Lewis had forgotten the Old Man's tales; had forgotten the link between the barman and the pool-player, would've been surprised to find out that the fat man's half-sister was a prostitute in Bristol. All Lewis could think was: Manon. Tomorrow. Two-thirty p.m. It became like the rhythm of a train in his head: Manon, tomorrow, two-thirty p.m. Manon, tomorrow, two-thirty p.m. A runaway train, an out-of-control train. A train he couldn't stop, even if he wanted to.

CHAPTER EIGHT

The next day, round about noon, Jonathan 'Cakes' Cunningham crossed over into Wales, over the Severn bridge. Half-way across the bridge he wanted to get out and admire the structure, the awesome feat of engineering that it represented, but of course he couldn't. Like all restrictions on his behaviour, this made him grit his teeth and grip the steering wheel tighter. *Angered* him slightly. He took the motorway past Newport and Cardiff and then Port Talbot, like a city of soot on his left with the glittering sea behind it. Richard Burton was born around here, he thought. Anthony Hopkins too. Strange how such talent can be born in such places, such dirty places, dusty and black and polluted. At Swansea he continued towards Carmarthen, where he had to pull into a lay-by to check directions. He took the crumpled envelope out of his pocket and smoothed it out on the dashboard. He tried to read the words, smudged with sweat. He could make out 'Ferryside'.

He drove on. At Ferryside he checked the directions again and took the road up into the hills. The ground rose around him, green and wooded. He began to feel a little uncomfortable, in his van on these high hills. He didn't trust the higher ground. He wanted to be back on a flat road again. Wanted to be back down at sea level, where he felt he belonged.

He entered a village, but he had a feeling it wasn't the one he was looking for. He stopped at the kerb outside a small general store and wound his window down. An old man came out of the shop carrying a loaf of bread and a two-pint plastic bottle of milk. Cakes beckoned him over.

'Scuse me, mate.'

The old man approached the van. 'Ga i'ch helpu chi?'

'Erm...d'you speak English?'

'Yes.'

'Good. I'm looking for this place.'

Cakes pointed to the place name written on the envelope. He didn't want to try and pronounce it – all those 'ch's and double 'l's. He'd make a fool of himself.

'Ah yes,' the old man said. 'You're not there yet. It's about another five miles that way.'

The old man pointed to a small lane, Cakes thanked him and took that lane. A tiny lane, barely wide enough for his van and hemmed in by high hedgerows. God knows what he'd do if he met any other traffic, he thought. But he didn't, and the next village he entered was the one he was looking for. He knew this without even consulting his directions; an affirmative feeling in his heart and stomach told him that this was the place where he'd get back what was his. There was a church on a hill and a shop and a garage and oh yes, look, a pub called the Miner's Arms. *This* was the place.

Cakes drove the van up the hill above the village and parked by the church where, he reasoned, neither he nor his van would be seen. He got out of the van and pulled his jacket tighter around him to keep the chill out and entered the churchyard where, to kill time, he read the inscriptions on the gravestones. He liked doing that, Cakes did; reading evidence of lives too short or lives too long although, in his more relaxed moments, he was of the opinion that *all* lives were too short. At a big marble headstone under a yew tree by the Garden of Rest he stopped and lit a cigarette while gazing out over the village below. Smoke rose from chimneys, the sound of some industrial machine came from the garage workshop. Little people were coming and going. A peaceful scene. A rural idyll, some might say, and despite himself Cakes felt his pulse slowing, felt his heartbeat calming. He felt at home amongst traffic and noise and crowds, but he had to admit to himself that here, in this little village in the middle of the hills, he didn't feel as angry as he usually did.

But still, he had things to do. If all went according to plan, if Smithy and Scottish Jim and Daft Larry and Parcelforce did their jobs properly, all Cakes would have to do would be to say a few words and bugger off again. Taking what belonged to him with him. It should all take care of itself. It should be easy. But he couldn't wait to see the look on that thieving bastard Lewis's face.

He checked his watch; nearly half past two. He left the churchyard and went down into the village. Towards the back room of the Miner's Arms.

It had been an interesting journey, over the past couple of days. And it wasn't over yet.

CHAPTER NINE

Thump thump thump went Lewis's heart. His mouth was dry and his palms were damp. His future and his happiness were about to be decided. It all depended on what another person would, in the next few minutes, tell him. The plans he'd made might be ashes in just a few minutes, and if so what would he do then? The possible life he'd built for himself might fall to bits. Never to be put back together again. Thump thump thump went his heart.

He went around the side of the pub, to the back door. Let himself in. There was Manon, sitting behind a table, looking beautiful. And next to her was the Old Man.

Lewis was surprised. 'What are you doing here? I don't need any support, y'know. I'm a big boy now.'

'Sit down, son,' the Old Man replied.

He pointed at a chair opposite Manon. Lewis took it. The table was now between him and Manon like a kind of barrier between them. He didn't like it.

'We've both got something to tell you, Lewis. Haven't we, love?'

Manon swallowed and nodded.

'So just be quiet and listen. Don't say a word until we've finished. Right?'

The Old Man nodded at Manon and sat back, lacing his fingers over his little pot belly. Manon cleared her throat. Her eyes were big and wide and had worry in them. Lewis sat still and listened and watched in wonder as the world spun out of control around him. He'd pictured a possible scene of damage and of heartbreak but *this*...this was a nightmare. Devastation.

'Remember I told you I'd spent time in London? That I lived in Swansea but spent a lot of time in London?'

Lewis felt himself nod once.

'Well, that wasn't quite true. See, I went to London in the first place to find you. I figured that's where you'd go. I knew you had friends there – you used to talk a lot about going there and I wanted to find you. I missed you, Lewis. Despite all that happened I missed you. Because the baby was yours too, y'know.'

Lewis felt himself nod again. His eyes burned.

'Plus I was worried that you might hurt

yourself or something so I went looking for you. Daft, I know, in a city that big, but...' She shrugged. 'I stayed in a friend's bedsit. Got a job delivering cakes around the Holborn area on a bike. It seemed strange right from the start – I mean, I was delivering doughnuts and cream slices and stuff to squats and tower blocks and places like that. Not shops or offices at lunchtime or anything. Just didn't seem right.'

Lewis's heart began to sink into his body. It plopped into his stomach.

'So she called me,' the Old Man said. 'Couldn't call her father 'cos he was still looking to blow your bloody brains out, so she called me. Said there was something fishy about the bakery she was working for. She sounded frightened so I went to Swansea and caught the first train to London.'

'I met him at Paddington,' Manon said. 'With a box full of éclairs that should've been delivered to a squat in Clerkenwell earlier that day. We went back to my bedsit and cut them open...I'm sure you can guess what we found.'

Lewis swallowed, although there was nothing to swallow. Just hot and stale air inside his mouth.

'So I went round to the bakery,' the Old Man said. 'Angry, like. Furious, I was. Innocent young girl being taken advantage of like that, not on. I was all up for teaching some bugger a lesson like, but in that bakery I met a feller who told me some *very* interesting things. Like who else was working for him. As a barman in a pub he owned, called the Queen's Head. Isn't that right, Cakes?'

The Old Man nodded at a spot above Lewis's head and Lewis spun in his seat. There he was. Just standing there and smiling down at him. Cakes, here in the Miner's Arms. Cakes here in Wales. Cakes, the rumoured killer, just standing there in the village where Lewis was born, where he still called home. Nowhere was safe.

The world spun around Lewis. Spun and fell apart.

Lewis's heart fell further.

'So we came to an arrangement,' Cakes said, perching himself on one arse cheek on the end of the table, next to Manon. 'That certain people kept shtum about my little bakery business and I, in return, kept watch over a certain barman. Made sure no harm came to him. Especially made sure that he stayed unfound by a certain shotgun-wielding feller from Wales, whose daughter had just had a miscarriage. Ring any bells? Understand what I'm saying, Lewis?'

Lewis couldn't take his eyes off Cakes's face. His hands were shaking. His heart was in his groin. He wanted to run.

'But why didn't you just...just...'

My God, was that his voice? That pathetic squeak?

'What, have them bumped off?' Cakes said, nodding his head sideways at Manon and the Old Man. 'Shut them up? Permanently, like?'

He smiled. 'Because I liked them. I warmed to them. And besides, I knew one day they'd come in handy.'

Cakes dug a creased and tatty envelope out of his pocket. 'Thanks for the directions,' he said, and both the Old Man and Manon nodded. Cakes balled the envelope up in his fist and tossed it at a bin in the corner. It bounced off the wall above and dropped in.

'Bull's eye. As good a shot with a ball of paper as you are with a fucking whisky bottle, Lewis, yeah?'

Cakes took his hat off and tilted his head so that they could all see the bump there. Like an egg, a maroon and blue egg, with yellowing around it. Black streaks of blood under the skin. Very colourful.

'*You* did that?' Manon asked Lewis, startled.

'Oh yes, he did,' Cakes answered, replacing

his baseball hat. 'He never told you about whacking me on the noggin with a whisky bottle, no? While he was stealing my money, like. Never told you about using violence, no?'

He looked at Lewis and shook his head sadly. 'Tut tut, Lewis. A liar as well? Dear oh dear oh dear.'

Manon and the Old Man stared at Lewis. Cakes leaned so that his face was just an inch or so from Lewis's. Lewis saw the tiny hairs up Cakes's nose, the red veins thinner than those hairs in the whites of his eyes. Smelled his breath, coffee and tobacco, bad.

'Just give me my fucking money back, Lewis. You thieving bastard. I should really take your fucking fingers off, but just give me what's mine and we'll say no more about it. I won't hurt you. Alright?'

Lewis couldn't speak. His heart had sunk into his crotch and he thought he might piss himself. Cakes stood upright.

'Where's the money, Lewis? *My* money. Where is it?'

'I know where it is,' Manon said. 'It's in a locker in the garage. I know where the spare keys are, too.'

'Good girl,' said Cakes. 'Knew I could rely on

you. Let's go and get it, eh?'

Manon stood. Went around the table to stand at Cakes's side. He put his arm around her waist and she leaned her head on his shoulder and looked, without smiling, at Lewis.

'Oh yes,' Cakes said. 'I forgot to ask. He *did* propose, did he? Was my hunch correct?'

Manon nodded. 'Yesterday. He wanted us to run off together to New York.'

Cakes laughed. 'How romantic. New York? Aw Christ. The dreams some people have!'

He kissed Manon on the cheek. 'I've missed you,' he said.

'And I've missed you,' she replied, still looking at Lewis, but talking to Cakes.

'Still want to go?'

'Where?'

'New York. To stay in that condo on the Upper East Side I bought last year.'

'Of course I do. There's nothing I'd like more.'

'Well let's go, then. Let's go and get my money back and then catch the first plane to the States. Goodbye, Lewis. Goodbye, William.'

He nodded at Lewis and the Old Man and turned to go with Manon. At the door Manon turned back and mouthed 'I'll write' at the Old Man and then stared at Lewis.

'You deserted me,' she said. 'You ran away when I needed you most. Don't you ever forget that. 'Cos I won't.'

And then she closed the door behind her.

The empty shell that was Lewis turned to face the Old Man. It looked like Lewis, it moved like Lewis, but it was just a shell. There were tears on its cheeks and a roaring in its head.

'What can I say, son?' William said. 'Never trust anybody. Everything's connected, just look for the signs. And never leave a woman when she needs you most. Nobody loves a coward.'

The Old Man rose and left. The world was rubble at Lewis's shoes.

He stared at the tabletop. He looked at the words carved into its surface, but didn't really read them. His heart went on beating and his lungs went on taking in air but he was no longer alive. He looked at his watch: 3 p.m. The hour of his death.

A knock at the door. He got up and answered it. A man in a uniform holding a huge wedding cake.

'Special delivery,' the man said. 'Congratulations. Where should I put it?'

Without waiting for Lewis to answer he walked over to the table and put the cake down on it. Then he congratulated Lewis again and left.

Such a big cake. A wedding cake. The tiny bride and groom on top of it held hands and had minuscule painted smiles on their tiny faces. The bride had long dark hair like Manon. The groom had short brown hair like Lewis. Maybe Manon had ordered this. Maybe she was coming back. Maybe this business of leaving with Cakes was just to teach Lewis a lesson. Maybe they were laughing outside the door and she was just about to come back in again and say she'd forgiven him really; that she wanted to marry him, yes, and she wanted to go to New York with him and not with Cakes and –

Some life came back into Lewis. He turned to face the door. He would be smiling when Manon came back through that door which he knew she would, any second now. He'd be smiling and ready to hug her. Ready to begin their new life.

He stood there smiling and waiting as the clock ticked on the wall. As the clock ticked many times.

Footsteps outside. The door handle turned. Here she was. Coming back to him. Bringing it back home.

67

The door swung inwards. Lewis smiled, holding his arms out wide.

CHAPTER TEN

'Do you want to do it or shall I?'

'I'll do it,' Manon said, holding the rucksack tightly to her stomach where it bulged like a pregnancy. 'My phone or yours?'

'Neither,' Cakes said. 'The call can be traced. We'll have to use a phone box.'

They drove down out of the hills and found a public phone box outside a chapel in a little village. Manon put the rucksack safely beneath the passenger seat and then she and Cakes got out of the van and crammed themselves into the phone box. She lifted the receiver and dialled 999. Asked for the police.

'Miner's Arms,' she said to the voice on the other end of the line. 'The back room there. There's a man in there with a wedding cake. Look inside the cake. You'll find something very interesting.'

'Miner's Arms?' the voice said. 'Whereabouts?'

She named the village, the place where she was born, where she got pregnant and lost the baby, the place she once called home.

'Thank you,' the voice said. 'I'll send someone round there right away. Can I ask who's calling? You could be in line for a Community Action Trust reward.'

Manon hung up and she and Cakes ran back into the van, laughing. Inside, Cakes turned the key and the engine barked into life. He and Manon leaned and kissed each other deep and long and then he drove away out of Wales, heading east, in the direction of Heathrow airport.

A DAY TO REMEMBER

BY FIONA PHILLIPS

ISBN 1905170904 / 9781905170906

price £1.99

A modern romantic comedy about love, loyalty and limos written by Fiona Phillips, GMTV presenter

A Day To Remember is a successful business but, when her right-hand man Steve runs away with their receptionist and the limo, Jo is left to pick up the pieces. Bookings are a mess, her home life's in chaos and then her son accidentally damages the new neighbour's Mercedes. Far from a Day To Remember it's turning into a week she'd just rather forget...

THE RUBBER WOMAN

BY LINDSAY ASHFORD

ISBN 1905170882 / 9781905170883

price £1.99

The world of Cardiff's sex trade hits the headlines when a woman is butchered and left for dead. Pauline distributes condoms to the women of the red light district and is known locally as 'the rubber woman'. She and Megan, a forensic psychologist, make it their mission to stop more women becoming victims. They don't know it yet, but one of them is already marked out for death.

AIM HIGH

BY DAME TANNI GREY THOMPSON

ISBN 1905170890 / 9781905170890
price £1.99

Aim High reveals what has motivated Dame Tanni Grey Thompson, UK's leading wheelchair athlete, through the highs and lows of her outstanding career. Her triumphs, which include winning 16 medals, eleven of which are gold, countless European titles, six London Marathons and over 30 world records have catapulted this Welsh wheelchair athlete firmly into the public consciousness.

THE CORPSE'S TALE

BY KATHERINE JOHN

ISBN 1905170319 / 9781905170319
price £2.99

Dai Morgan has the body of a man and the mind of a child. He lived with his mother in the Mid Wales village of Llan, next door to bright, beautiful 19 year old Anna Harris. The vicar found Anna's naked, battered body in the churchyard one morning. The police discovered Anna's bloodstained earring in Dai's pocket.

The judge gave Dai life.

After ten years in gaol Dai appealed against his sentence and was freed. Sergeants Trevor Joseph and Peter Collins are sent to Llan to reopen the case. But the villagers refuse to believe Dai innocent. The Llan police do not make mistakes or allow murderers to walk free.

Do they?

SECRETS

BY LYNNE BARRETT-LEE

ISBN 1905170300 / 9781905170302

price £2.99

Sisters Megan and Ffion have never had secrets, so when Megan goes to flat-sit all she's expecting is a rest and a change.

When a stranger called Jack phones, Megan wonders who he is. Ffion behaves like she's just seen a ghost, and refuses to say any more.

So is Jack a ghost? Ffion's not telling and when she disappears too, and the mystery deepens. Megan begins to fear for the future. She's always been the one who's looked after her little sister. Is this going to be the one time she can't?